In the Back Seat

Deborah Durland DeSaix

Farrar · Straus · Giroux New York

For Hilary,
sister extraordinaire

Ariel and her little brother, Jeffrey, climbed into the back seat of the family car.

"Are we there yet?" Jeffrey asked.

"Almost," said Mom, laughing.

"In a few minutes," said Dad, starting the car.

"Are you guys nuts?" asked Ariel. "Jeffrey, we're going to Aunt Penelope's farm way out in the country. It'll take a while."

"I don't want to leave home," Jeffrey said. "Besides, I'm too short to see anything back here."

"You can see the sky, can't you?" asked Ariel. "Doesn't that cloud look like Mr. Karansky sitting on the stoop?"

"I think it looks more like his dog, Rocky," said Jeffrey.

"Hey, what's that speck up there in front of Rocky?" Jeffrey asked, pointing.

Ariel squinted. "It looks like a girl and her pesky little brother to me. Flying."

"What!" shouted Jeffrey.

"Flying. In a balloon," she insisted. "They're going on a trip through the country."

"Uh-oh," he said. "They're flying into
a big dark cloud."

"Well, they're going to have to land,"
Ariel said firmly.

"They've disappeared," Jeffrey said.
"No, they just fell into a haystack."
"What's a haystack?" he asked.
"It's a big pile of hay. It looks like
Mrs. O'Malley's hair. Especially the one
that they fell into," she added.

"Are they all right?"

"I think so," Ariel said. "I can't see them now. They're in the middle of a cornfield. It goes on for miles and the corn's really tall."

"As tall as our apartment building?"

"Maybe even taller. Wait, there they are!" she said.

"Now they've come to the end of the cornfield and climbed the fence," said Ariel. "They're in a field. There's grass and flowers and . . . cows! I think the cows want to eat them."

"Lots of cows?"

"Lots," she answered, "and I didn't know cows were so big. Ohhh, I see. Hay is stuck in their clothes. That's what the cows want."

"What are they doing now?" Jeffrey asked, yawning.

"Her brother needs a nap," Ariel said. "The smallest cow let him climb on its back and the girl's leading it while he sleeps. Do you want to take a nap, too?"

"No way. I'll miss something."

"Okay, squirt. They've stopped at a river. The cow's staying behind."

"That was a nice cow," Jeffrey said.

"The girl and her brother are jumping from rock to rock across the river," said Ariel. "Wait a minute! Those aren't rocks, they're turtles! They're snapping at the little boy."

"Yikes!" said Jeffrey. "I don't think I like turtles."

"They got away," said Ariel. "The girl
and her brother jumped onto a log that
was floating by. Turtles aren't very fast."

"Thank goodness," Jeffrey said.
"Where did they float to?"

"They jumped off at the riverbank. There are trees all around. I think it's a forest."

"Are they going in there?"

"Yes. But it's dark and creepy. There's no telling what kind of animals or things there might be. It would be scary to walk through it. They're climbing into a big tree."

"I like to climb trees in the park, but it makes me hungry," Jeffrey said. "Let's eat."

"Okay," said Ariel. "Oh no! Spiders, in the trees! Big ones."

"How do the boy and his sister get away?"

"They crawl through the branches with their sweaters pulled over their heads. The spiders think that they're spiders, too, and leave them alone."

"That's really smart," said Jeffrey, taking a bite of his cookie.

"They got through the forest and now they're climbing down a cliff to the valley. They're so high up that a hawk is flying right around them. Hey! The hawk just turned and zoomed over and grabbed the boy by the sweater!"

"The hawk's hungry," Jeffrey shrieked. "The boy should give it the rest of his cookie!"

"Great idea," Ariel shouted. "He's taking it out of his pocket. The hawk's eating it! The hawk let him go!"

"They're going to be okay now, aren't they?" Jeffrey asked.

"They're going to be fine," Ariel said.

"We're here!" their mother sang out. "Aunt Penelope's farm!" Aunt Penelope waved from the front porch. Ariel and Jeffrey climbed out of the back seat.

"Some adventure, huh?" Ariel said.

"Whew," Jeffrey answered. "I can't believe we made it."